Only the best cadets become

Don't miss a single mission!

#1 Alien Attack

#2 Deadly Mission

Coming soon:

#3 The Enemy's Lair

#4 Crash Landing

MAX CHASE

BLOOMSBURY

NEW YORK BERLIN LONDON SYDNEY

Text copyright © 2012 by Working Partners Limited
Illustrations copyright © 2012 by Sam Hadley
All rights reserved. No part of this book may be reproduced or transmitted in any form
or by any means, electronic or mechanical, including photocopying, recording, or by any
information storage and retrieval system, without permission in writing from the publisher.

First published in Great Britain in February 2012 by Bloomsbury Publishing Plc
First published in the United States of America in May 2012
by Bloomsbury Books for Young Readers
www.bloomsburykids.com

For information about permission to reproduce selections from this book, write to
Permissions, Bloomsbury BFYR, 175 Fifth Avenue, New York, New York 10010

Library of Congress Cataloging-in-Publication Data
available upon request
ISBN 978-1-59990-850-2

Typeset by Hewer Text UK Ltd., Edinburgh
Printed in the U.S.A. by Quad/Graphics, Fairfield, Pennsylvania
2 4 6 8 10 9 7 5 3 1

All papers used by Bloomsbury Publishing, Inc., are natural, recyclable products
made from wood grown in well-managed forests. The manufacturing processes
conform to the environmental regulations of the country of origin.

J F CHA
1640 5212 5/14/12 LJB
Chase, Max.

Star fighters
          ABJ

Special thanks to Tom Genrich and Michele Perry

LeRoy Collins Leon Co.
Public Library System
200 West Park Avenue
Tallahassee, FL 32301

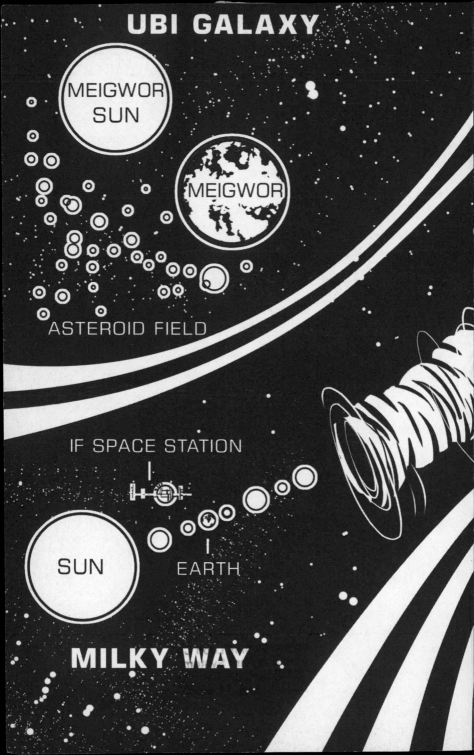

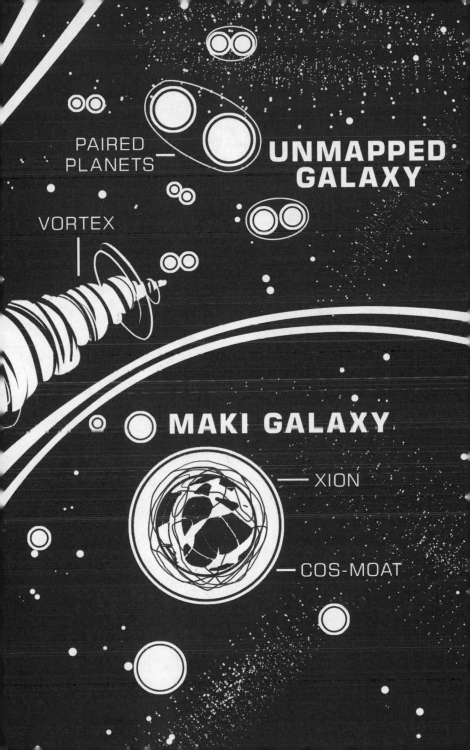

STAR FIGHTERS

An elite fighting team sworn to protect and defend the galaxy

It's the year 5012 and the Milky Way galaxy is under attack . . .

After the Universal War—a war that almost brought about the destruction of every known universe—the planets in the Milky Way banded together to create the Intergalactic Force, an elite fighting team sworn to protect and defend the galaxy.

Only the brightest and most promising eleven-year-olds are accepted into the Intergalactic Force Academy, and only the very best cadets reach the highest of their ranks and become . . .

To be a Star Fighter is to dedicate your life to one mission: Peace in Space. Star Fighters are given the coolest weapons, the fastest spaceships—and the most dangerous missions. Everyone at the Intergalactic Force Academy wants to be a Star Fighter someday.

Do you have what it takes?

Chapter 1

"Eat dust, alien invader!" Peri shouted as the asteroid shattered into a million glittery pieces.

This sure beats the simulator, he thought as he swerved left then jetted upward to avoid the asteroid's fiery remains.

He was millions of miles from the Intergalactic Force Space Station and even farther from planet Earth. Up ahead was a bright-blue planet surrounded by shimmering ice rings... Saturn! Peri could barely believe his eyes.

Ping! The sonar let him know that their last target was within firing range. It wasn't as good as saving Earth from an alien attack, but blowing up cosmic trash was still way better than any 3-D game he'd ever played. He'd blasted an ancient TV satellite and zapped an old rocket booster. And that asteroid had been totally obliterated.

"Try to keep the pod steady this time, you lamizoid," Diesel said.

Peri glanced over at Diesel, who was swiveling the D-Stroy lasers in the weapon turret. He noticed the gunner wasn't wearing his astro-harness, so any sudden turn would knock the big lug right off his seat. Peri grinned. He banked as hard as he could. "Woo-hooo!"

Whack-slam! Diesel flipped out of his seat. "*Ch'ach!*" he shouted. Diesel always spoke his native language when he was angry—which

was most of the time. The gunner's yellow eyes were flashing. The band of hair that stretched across his head was bristling. When he was mad, Diesel looked more Martian than human, though in fact he was both.

"You made me miss my target!" he yelled. "I told them to give me a second-year pilot. But instead, I get a newbie who knows less than nothing!"

"Chill," Peri said. "I'll get us back on track."

Peri chuckled to himself. A few bruises served Diesel right. That morning he had thrown a galactic fit when he and Peri were paired for a rare Intergalactic Force Academy training mission. The half-Martian was a second-year cadet, a weapons ace, and a 3-D gaming champion, but he wasn't the brightest star in the constellation.

Peri agreed with Diesel about one thing—it was odd that a first-year IFA cadet had been chosen. And Peri wasn't even the best in his year; he ranked fourteenth in rocket science and tenth in cosmic combat. So why *had* they selected him?

During the past two weeks he'd pretty much lived in the flight simulator. He practiced over and over again until his vision became blurry. But nothing could compare with the real thing—looping the rings of Saturn or whipping around Pluto.

Suddenly, the pod jerked sharply to the left. Peri's astro-harness snapped him to his seat. Peri struggled to regain control of the steering as the pod looped in a broad U-turn and accelerated.

"What's happening?" Peri's fingers darted over the screens. He engaged the flight stabilizer, checked the energy gauge, and tapped the hologram route finder. "Nothing's working," he called to Diesel. "It's like somebody else is controlling the pod!"

"They must be bringing you back to the space station," Diesel jeered. "I bet you're in trouble for that silly stunt you—"

But before he could finish, the pod rocked again, even more violently than before. There was a dull thud beside Peri.

"*Aaargh!*" Diesel roared in pain as he staggered back to his seat clutching his chin. "*I bib ma dung!*"

Peri ignored him. He had much bigger things to worry about.

His muscles strained as he wrestled with the antidrift levers, trying to keep the pod on a steady course while it was batted around like a spaceball. His eyes were drawn to a flashing light on the control board—the red light that signaled a problem with the nuke-fusion engine. His ears rattled with the piercing robotic voice that warned: "Danger! Temperature shield overheating. Danger!"

Between jolts, he was able to flip on his com-unit. "Mayday! Mayday!" he called. "IF Space Station—this is TP2-7. Do you copy?"

There was no reply. All Peri heard was a rush of static.

Then, as they rounded Mars, Peri saw something that made his heart nearly rocket

out of his chest. Dea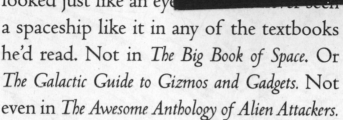
roadblock, was a me
Earth's moon. As he
of large spikes spro
They were razor sha
each spike was a vi
looked just like an ey
a spaceship like it in any of the textbooks
he'd read. Not in *The Big Book of Space*. Or
The Galactic Guide to Gizmos and Gadgets. Not
even in *The Awesome Anthology of Alien Attackers*.

Diesel started yelling in a mixture of
Martian and English.

Peri gulped down his fear. "B-buckle
up . . . and shut up!" he snapped.

"You don't give the orders around here!
I'm the—" Diesel stopped and gawked at
the alien ship. "*S'fâh*," he muttered. "That's
not from this galaxy." Diesel scrambled back
to his seat and, finally, strapped himself in.

All the navigation systems said the same thing: they were on a collision course with the alien vessel.

"I can't stop the pod!" Peri shouted. "We're going to crash!"

Chapter 2

The pod hurtled toward the alien ship. Peri and Diesel were helpless. They could only stare in horror as hatches opened on the biggest spikes, revealing mighty pulverizers. Each pulverizer was studded with laser barrels, their tips glowing molten red with heat.

"DeathRays!" they shouted together.

All of the deadly lasers were aimed at a familiar blue-and-white planet in the distance.

Planet Earth.

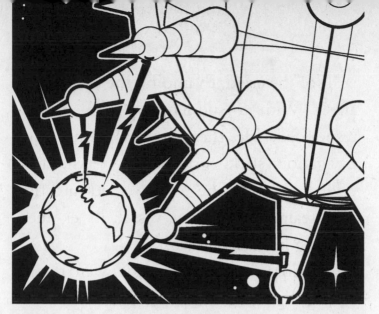

The guns let loose with an almighty *boom!*
Lances of fire lit up the darkness as the
laser beams streaked straight toward Earth.
When they reached their target, there was a
huge flash of white, hot light. Earth's force
field sizzled and sparked as it absorbed
most of the blow. For a moment, Peri
thought the planet might survive, but the
force field began to pulse with a dull red
glow. The glow turned to a hazy purple.
Peri balled his hands into fists.

"No!" he cried, thumping the console in anger. With a sudden *beep!* the system responded. He threw himself onto the navigation stick, gritted his teeth, and pulled up hard. The pod swerved into the slipstream of the giant vessel, its engines howling like a space-wolf.

The closest eyeball swiveled toward them. Orange light beamed out and scanned their pod from side to side. Peri's pulse was racing like a turbo engine. Then the socket rotated away again.

"Uh, why aren't they firing on us?" Diesel asked.

"I guess we don't worry them," Peri replied.

"*Ýṇoĝr!*" Diesel shouted. "I have a ninety-nine percent hit rate. I'm the best cadet gunner in IF history—and they're not even worried! Well, I'll show them!"

"Yeah, those dumboids are making a big mistake," Peri hissed. "No one attacks Earth." As the alien ship fired on Earth again, he used the pod's radar to pinpoint the nearest pulverizer.

"Diesel," he called over his shoulder. "Ready to dish out some payback?"

"Bring it on!" the half-Martian yelled. Peri heard him cracking his knuckles.

"Target is enemy pulverizer!" said Peri. "Uploading coordinates to you now."

"Roger that!" his gunner replied. "Locked and loaded. We'll blast them into outer space!"

Peri took a deep breath and tried not to panic. He knew they did not have enough firepower to do that. They had taken off that morning equipped for target practice, not for an all-out battle. But if he could get their pod close enough and aim just right, then maybe they could buy Earth some time.

Peri skillfully steered the pod to within a few hundred space-meters of the pulverizer. "Ready and . . . *fire!*"

Diesel's lasers streaked toward their target. There was a blinding flash. An instant later a giant fireball exploded from one side of the enemy ship. Chunks of burning metal rained on the cadets' pod, clanging loudly.

"Yes!" Peri punched the air. "Nice shooting, gunner!"

Diesel smiled a rare smile. "Not bad steering either, newbie."

Then they froze.

Diesel cleared his throat. "Um, do you see what I'm seeing?"

Peri let out a low groan. A fighter jet had emerged from the other side of the alien warship. It was heading straight for them. The pod's warning lights began to flash.

"He's locked onto us!" Peri was light-years beyond fear and fast approaching all-out panic. A pod couldn't outrun—or outgun—a fighter jet armed with cluster missiles. He closed his eyes and braced for an impact that would blow his pod to pieces.

The explosion made his ears ring and his blood tingle, but there was no burning pain. Instead there was just a fizzing sensation, as if he were a well-shaken bottle of Saturn Soda.

Wait! I know that feeling.

His eyes flew open. They'd been transported back to the IF Space Station!

"Phew! They beamed us down just in time," he said shakily. He pulled off his flight tags and loosened the collar of his

uniform. "I guess the pod is history, though."

Diesel said something, but his words were lost in the blaring of sirens. The launch bay was swarming with activity, looking like an anthill someone had rammed with a stick. Ground staff and flight crews were running this way and that. Spaceships, fighter jets, and troop carriers were jostling for takeoff. The noise was deafening.

The intercom boomed. "All personnel to battle stations. Engage LR Scenario. Repeat: Engage LR Scenario!"

Immediately, two Intergalactic Force sergeants rushed toward the boys. Peri and Diesel stood to attention. "IFA cadets reporting for duty," Diesel said in his deepest voice. The sergeants grabbed them like a couple of empty spacesuits and hauled them away from the action.

"Hey, wait!" Diesel protested, legs kicking

the air. "I was the one who took out their pulverizer. I'm the best gunner in cadet history! I want to stay and fight! Do you know who I am?"

Peri struggled to free himself. He had to do something. He couldn't be sidelined as some alien bullies attacked his galaxy. But the sergeants held on to them tightly as they marched to an empty corner of the launch bay.

"Where—" Peri began, but he couldn't finish his question. The next thing he knew, he was being thrown clear off his feet by a shock wave from an explosion.

Smack! Peri crashed into something hard and slid to the floor.

"Ahhh . . . ," he groaned, sitting up slowly and looking around for whatever it was he'd hit. But there was nothing. Had he imagined it? He groped the air. His fingertips touched something cold and sleek—but *invisible*. He blinked with disbelief.

He slid his hands over the invisible surface. Some sort of force field fizzled around his skin, flickering a few times.

"Whoa!" Peri started, but his brain had no words for what was coming into focus.

It was unbelievable.

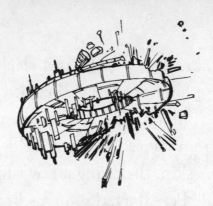

Chapter 3

The spaceship seemed to appear by magic in front of Peri. It must have been there all along, hidden by some sort of cloaking device. The vessel was shaped like an egg and glittered like a thousand stars. Its shell was smooth; Peri couldn't see a single door, window, rivet, or joint. He couldn't even see where the engine would go.

One of the sergeants pulled Peri to his feet and forced Peri's hand onto the ship's sparkling surface. A ghostly green light traced his palm, and he felt a prickly sensation as it gently scanned his flesh and bones. Instantly, a rectangle-shaped outline appeared. Diesel and the other sergeant had to scramble out of the way as a door swung open and a ramp glided to the floor. Bright light flooded out from the vessel. Peri looked over at Diesel. The second-year gunner stood openmouthed, looking just as stunned as Peri was.

The sergeant gave them both a hard shove. "Get in!" he barked. The two boys stumbled aboard.

"Last Resort Scenario has been engaged," said the other sergeant. Then he stood to attention and saluted. "You have your orders."

"Uh, no, we don't, sir," Peri objected as the door snapped shut and immediately blended back into the wall, leaving no trace of an opening. He fumbled, looking for some kind of switch or handle, but there was nothing.

"Well, they must have put us in here for a reason, right?" Peri said more to himself than to Diesel. "Come on, let's get this thing fired up so we can join in the fight."

"Oh yeah," Diesel grunted.

They raced up the stairs in front of them and found themselves in a corridor with smooth white sides and mauve strip-lighting. Everything looked brand new, as if it had only just been built. A moving walkway started with a hum as soon as they stepped onto it.

Robotic arms shot out of the walls and grabbed both boys. Diesel struggled, but the steel arms held them securely in tight pinch-grips. Peri was lifted up and lowered into coveralls. He heard the strange garment clicking, and a rustling as it tightened.

Something solid was slipped onto his feet. Then the robotic arms released them.

Peri looked down at himself. "Check it out!" he exclaimed. "Temperature-adjust suits! Mine's already turning blue with the heat from my body. And real space boots with magnetic soles, in case we lose gravity. This is shrink-to-fit Expedition Wear!"

"It's almost as if the ship was waiting for us," Diesel said, looking at his own jacket in wonder. When the walkway whirred up again, the half-Martian sprinted toward the double doors up ahead. They slid open at just the right moment, so he didn't even have to break his stride. But he skidded to a halt anyway.

"*Oof!*" Peri gasped, as he slammed into Diesel.

The two boys stood gazing in awe at what was spread out before them.

The ship's bridge!

Peri could feel its power. The room was oval and so vast you could have parked a whole fleet of training pods inside it. Every surface shone like polished moonstone. When Peri moved closer, he realized that the walls were actually floor-to-ceiling 360-monitors. All at once, they pulsed into life. He could see the launch bay outside so clearly it was like looking through windows.

Then he spotted a wedge shape that hovered in midair in front of the screens. "The control panel!" he exclaimed and raced over to it. It was covered in dozens of mysterious buttons and levers and nano-dials.

A hologram appeared above the panel. On it were written two letters and three numbers. Peri had to read them twice before he could really take them in: LR-999. He was inside the fastest and most advanced spaceship ever

built! In fact, it was nineteen times faster, thirty-five times more advanced, and about a gazillion times cooler than even an imperial star cruiser.

"Wow!" he whispered. "It's the *Phoenix* . . ."

Diesel elbowed him to one side. His eyes lit up. "*Klûu'ah*," he said in a hushed voice. "I always thought the *Phoenix* was just a myth."

"I knew it was real." The words were out before Peri could stop himself. The existence of the *Phoenix* was super top secret; Peri was absolutely not supposed to know about this ship. But several times he'd overheard his parents whispering about it. They were the highest-ranking astronautical engineers with the IF, and they had worked on upgrading the legendary ship.

Diesel gave him a sidelong look. "Yeah, well . . . I've known about the *Phoenix* my whole life," he boasted.

Peri shrugged. He didn't have time for Diesel's games. If he could work out how to operate the *Phoenix*, then maybe he and Diesel could help save planet Earth—or at least save themselves. He studied the control panel, with its maze of buttons, but it didn't faze him. He felt strangely calm.

Eeeeeeeeeeeeeeeeeee! He jumped as an alarm rang out. Two chairs sprang up from the floor, knocking into the boys' knees and forcing them to sit down. Floating astro-harnesses appeared, crisscrossing just in front of their bodies. Immediately, the ground shifted and Peri's stomach lurched like he was going to be sick.

"What did you do, you cosmic wastoid?" Diesel barked.

"Nothing. I swear." Peri scanned the control panel and gulped. "I think we're lifting off!"

As the ship went into launch mode, he could feel the engine's vibrations even through the magnetic soles of his space boots. The lights of the bridge dimmed. The monitors started to glow, and within seconds the shell of the *Phoenix* had become completely see-through. Outside, the domed roof of the launch bay slid open. Now there was nothing between them and outer space. The calm, measured voice of the computer filled the bridge. "Good luck to you both," she said. "Peace in Space."

With an almighty surge, the *Phoenix* took off. Peri didn't have time to say a word before it shot out into space.

Then everything became still.

For once, Diesel was at a loss for words too.

On the screens in front of them, the alien warship loomed large, spikes out, hatches wide open. Thousands of tentacles sprang from the openings. They whipped through space and attached themselves to Earth's force field. A deafening hum like a mega turbo engine rattled the air and made Peri's eardrums vibrate.

"What are they doing?" Diesel asked.

"Looks like they're trying to destroy Earth's force field." Peri watched as the tubes sparked white and then glowed violet. Cracks snaked through the planet's force field until the green and blue forms underneath blurred.

Moments later, millions of armed fighter jets swarmed out of the alien ship. Each one took a different course, speeding to all corners of the galaxy.

"The entire Milky Way is under attack!" Diesel said, horrified.

"We've got to do something!" Peri shouted. He twisted wildly in his chair, but the floating astro-harness shadowed his every move, keeping him seated.

Just then, a monitor set into the control panel began to flicker. On the grainy screen the image of a man with a tired face and short white hair blinked in and out.

"General Pegg!" Peri cried.

The head of the IF Star Fighters was desperately trying to contact them. "Peri! . . . *Crrrk* . . . *crrrk* . . . Peri, can you—"

Boooom! An explosion in the background made the general flinch. Dirt and debris rained down on him. He spluttered and wiped his eyes, spitting dust out of his mouth. Sirens were wailing.

The boys strained forward to hear him over the noise. "Our Space Station . . . under atta— . . . *crrrrk* . . . aliens . . . *sssssss-boom!* . . . from planet Xion . . ." General Pegg fixed his eyes on Peri. The transmission cleared for a moment, and his voice came through in a rush. "Peri, your mission is to take Emperor Elliotte's son to safety. The *Phoenix* was built for this very purpose—to save—*ra-ta-ta-ta-tac!*—in case of—*crrrrk*—a Universal War—"

The monitor went black, then disappeared into the control panel.

"Wait, come back!" Peri pleaded. His thoughts were scrambled. "Why *me*? Take

who to safety? How am I supposed to fly the *Phoenix*?"

There was no time for answers. As he watched, the alien warship readied its weapons again. This time, though, it turned its awesome firepower on the Intergalactic Force Space Station.

"Noooooooooo!" Diesel roared.

Countless DeathRays and cluster missiles flashed through the sky. The space station exploded into a cloud of galactic confetti.

Chapter 4

"What are you two idiots waiting for? An imperial invitation?" a high-pitched voice demanded from behind Peri and Diesel. Peri twisted around to see a girl about his own age standing with her hands on her hips. She looked familiar. He was pretty sure he'd seen her around the space station, though she wasn't a cadet.

The girl marched toward them and said, "We've got to get out of here!" When the boys didn't move, she rolled her eyes and punched a button on the control panel.

Peri and Diesel's astro-harnesses uncrossed and slipped away.

Peri blew out his cheeks in relief. "Hey, thanks!"

"Who in the grim galaxy are you?" Diesel growled at the girl.

"I'm Selene," she replied, pushing her hair back from her face. "I—"

Diesel cut her off: "And how did you sneak onboard our ship?"

Selene snorted. "I've practically lived on the *Phoenix* since I was old enough to crawl. So it's more *my* ship than yours."

Selene's spacesuit was patched at the knees. A tool belt hung around her waist. There was a smudge of oil on her cheek.

"Oh, really?" Diesel sneered. "And where have you been hiding, in the garbage unit?"

Selene jutted out her chin. "Actually, I've

just been fine-tuning the accelerator modules. My dad . . . he's an, umm . . . he's an IF technician, so—"

"So nothing. You're a stowaway!" Diesel said. "The Milky Way is under attack and we're cadets on a military mission. Anyway, *I'm* the oldest, so *I'm* in charge."

Peri ignored them and turned to the control panel. The space station was gone. Who knew if there were any survivors? They had to manage this ship by themselves now. He swept his hands over the console buttons. They started buzzing. He felt like a magnetic force was surging through him, pulling his fingers toward a pyramid-shaped button. It was bizarre, but he was sure it would activate the engine.

Kapow!

Before he had a chance to press the button, a burst of light and a deafening bang knocked them all to the floor. Peri was lying in a dazed heap. He heard snarling and hissing.

Selene shouted a warning: "Intruders!"

"*Mo'haa naroch!*" Diesel bellowed, jumping to his feet.

Peri scrambled up. Three aliens had beamed onboard!

The creatures towered over them. Their eyes bulged, their mouths gaped, and their antennae twitched. Their arms were covered in bristles, and their chests were armored in hard black shells. Instead of hands they had pincher claws.

The aliens bellowed in a strange accent: "For Xion!"

All three intruders rushed straight at Diesel. He was already crouched in the cosmic-combat attack position. When the first alien reached him, Diesel arched back,

spun around on one foot, and whipped the other through the air like a laser blade. The creature's legs were knocked out from under it. Down it crashed, cracking its shell. Underneath, Peri thought he saw a humanlike body. Were his attackers wearing suits to make them look scary?

"*Mars 'rakk!*" Diesel roared triumphantly. He readied himself for the next alien, legs braced and muscles flexed. "Bring it on, you cosmic cretins."

Peri lunged for the control panel. His right hand flipped a lever to activate the ship's defense shield. His left hand spun a zip-dial for the cloaking device. At least that would stop any more unwanted aliens beaming onboard. Then he leaped into the fray.

"*Aaargh!*" he yelled. The nearest alien had spun around and swiped at Peri's head. Peri flung up an arm in defense. A jagged claw tore through his sleeve and slashed his skin. The pain was intense, but he managed to yank his arm free. Blood was soaking into his shirt. The attacker had been knocked off balance, and now he pitched forward right into the hardest kick Peri had ever given.

Smash!

He felt like he was taking a spaceball penalty—while wearing magnetically reinforced boots. The creature bounced off his foot and crumpled.

Peri's head was zinging. He felt invincible. "You keep those two down," he called to Diesel. "I'll see to this one!" He turned to face the last intruder. To Peri's horror, a scorpion's tail sprang from the back of its black shell. The tail reared up high and rattled, ready to strike. Peri was rooted to the spot. Without a weapon, he didn't stand a chance . . .

Then he saw Selene. She was armed with the most amazing neon vaporizer Peri had ever laid eyes on. It looked lethal, with three gleaming titanium barrels and a galactoscopic sight . . . and she was aiming it straight at the alien.

"All right, you Xion creep," she said through gritted teeth. "Step away from the human!"

The alien backed up, hissing and spitting. But all of a sudden it flicked its deadly tail—at *Diesel*. Selene fired. A neon beam flashed across the room and struck with lightning force. The creature blazed white, shook violently, then faded into thin air. Every molecule had been vaporized.

"Nice shot!" Peri exclaimed. Diesel's mouth hung open.

The other two aliens were staring at Selene's vaporizer. Then they looked at each other and hit the orange buttons on the bands strapped just above their pinchers. A nanosecond later they were gone.

"They've beamed off," Diesel said in disgust. "What a bunch of cowards!" He slumped into his chair.

Selene flung the vaporizer to one side. Before it clattered onto the floor, mechanical arms sprang from the ceiling to catch it, clean it, and stow it away.

The girl jumped into the other chair. "Come on!" she urged Peri. "We've got to get out of here, *now!*"

Despite everything, Peri found himself grinning. "No problem!" He raised a finger, and the control panel glided through the air to settle in his hands. He pressed the pyramid-shaped button again. The engine started to hum. A third chair unfolded from the floor. Peri sat down . . . and the *Phoenix* took off. He set them on a straight course for the edge of the solar system.

"Okay," he said, putting the control panel aside, "we need a plan. First, let's find out if the ship has been damaged. Selene, can you do that?" She nodded and grabbed her tool belt. "Next," he continued, "we have to figure out everything about the *Phoenix*— how fast it can go, what weapons it has. And then," Peri slammed his fist into his palm, "we go back to fight!" He held up his hand for Diesel to high-five.

But Diesel shook his head. "Nope! The general ordered you to get us to safety, and that's exactly what you're going to do."

Peri stared at him. "You're kidding! You want us to run away? Anyway, General Pegg said I had to get the emperor's son to safety, and since he's clearly not onboard . . ." His voice trailed off.

Diesel was straightening up with a smug smile. The band of hair that stretched across his head glowed royal purple.

"Oh no," Peri groaned.

"Oh yes," said Diesel. "I'm Diaxo Samuel Elliotte the Tenth, heir to the imperial throne." He paused. "But you two can still call me Diesel, for short."

Selene raised her eyebrows and cocked her head.

Peri felt sick. Of all the people in the universe, why did it have to be Diesel? He sighed. Well, if he had to protect him, at least he would do it his way. And they sure weren't going to run away from evil aliens.

"I'm piloting this ship," he challenged, "and I say we go back and fight!"

"Yeah, well, I seriously outrank you," Diesel shot back. "So you'd better obey me!"

"Selene," Peri asked, "what's your vote?"

But there was no reply. Selene's face was deathly pale, and she was pointing at the viewing panel.

"VORTEX!" she cried.

Chapter 5

Alarms thundered all over the *Phoenix*: "VORTEX ALERT! VORTEX ALERT!"

Peri was stunned. Diesel grunted in surprise. On the 360-monitor in front of them loomed the ultimate peril: a huge cosmic whirlpool. Peri remembered his one training session on Hazards and Horrors in Space. The three most danger-ous threats to a spaceship were a meteorite shower, an alien attack, or a vortex.

And a vortex was the deadliest danger in the whole universe. Nothing could survive it.

They stared hopelessly at the spiraling current ahead. That same moment a Xion spaceship zoomed straight out of its churning center. The vessel's spikes and eyeballs were retracted, and its hatches were shut tight. It looked like a smooth orb of solid metal as it sped across the starry sky.

"But that's impossible!" Selene exclaimed.

Peri muttered, "Our instructor said that all machinery explodes or burns up . . ."

Diesel finished his sentence, " . . . when sucked into a vortex!"

"Correction," the *Phoenix*'s voice said softly. "Human-made machinery always explodes or burns up when sucked into a vortex."

"Those slime-eating Xion bugonauts!" Diesel shouted. "So *that's* how they were able to ambush the Milky Way. They came through the vortex!" He pounded his fists together. "I'll make 'em pay, if it's the last thing I do . . ."

The *Phoenix* seemed to be listening, because Peri saw a floating console appear in front of them. It had a 3-D target tracker, a row of triggers, and ten X-plode detonators. The gunnery station! Diesel made a dive for it.

The ship lurched forward. They were being drawn into the vortex with overwhelming force, like a moth to a solar flare.

"Okay," Peri said, his piloting instincts taking over. "Selene, you steer. Try to hold us steady."

"Don't worry about me," she quipped, springing into action. "I just hope the two of you know what *you're* doing!"

Peri reached for the turbo-reverse and anti-drift levers, and pulled using every atom of his strength.

But they wouldn't budge.

He slammed on the dodge mechanism and hyperbrakes. Nothing worked. He couldn't change the *Phoenix*'s course by a single space-meter.

Zing! Zing-zing! Laser beams were ricocheting off the defense shield. Peri saw that the Xion warship was fast approaching on their left flank. Its DeathRay pulverizers fired round after round.

But Diesel was ready. He had locked the 3-D tracker. He homed in on what the computer said was the enemy's munitions store. Now he let loose a volley of xenon missiles. They scored a direct hit. A huge explosion sent fireballs and mangled machinery spewing out of the Xion ship's hatches.

"˘*Grˉa-hin*," Diesel gloated.

"Yeah!" Peri yelled, even though he had no idea what Diesel meant.

An instant later the smile slid from his face. The vortex was so close it completely filled the *Phoenix's* monitors. As the terrified crew watched, a nearby asteroid was swallowed up and burned to ashes. A star the size of a space station followed.

There was no way to escape the vortex.

Selene frowned. "Hold on to your astroharnesses. There's only one way out of this mess," she said. And then Peri heard her mutter under her breath: "But it probably won't work."

Selene gripped the controls so tightly her knuckles turned white. And then she accelerated.

"What in Neptune's name are you *doing*?!" Peri wheezed, as he was thrust back into his seat by their speed.

Selene kept her eyes fixed on the velocity-viewer. "I'm going to set the ship to superluminal speed. If we're fast enough, we might just be able to power through the vortex without exploding."

"Nothing can go superluminal," Diesel said.

"The *Phoenix* was built for it, but it's never been tested," Selene replied. "And it takes a lot of power, so we'll only get one shot."

"You're going to fly into the vortex?" Peri cried.

"Why not?" Selene said, scanning the control panel. "What have we got to lose?"

The *Phoenix* began to rock in the strong astronomical current. All around it stars, asteroids, comets, and meteors were being sucked into the vortex. They blew up in multicolored fires.

Peri knew that, even at top speed, the odds of them surviving were less than nothing.

But they couldn't give up. So much depended on them: the mission General Pegg had given them, the future of the IF—maybe even the outcome of this Universal War. They had to keep trying, no matter what the odds.

"All right," Peri said, "initiate superluminal speed. It's our only chance. And who knows," he added hopefully, "if we make it, maybe we can stop more Xion ships from invading."

Selene cleared her throat. "There's just one problem."

"Oh, here we go," Diesel said. "What now, whiz kid?"

Selene gave him a withering look. "I've figured out a lot of the controls by myself, but I've always been on the *Phoenix* when it's grounded, so—"

"So you don't actually know how to take us to superluminal," Diesel scoffed. "Well, that's just great!"

The ship was already looping the outermost rim of the vortex. Peri took a deep breath and studied the control panel, concentrating harder than ever before. A smooth red section caught his attention. He flattened his palm over it, heard a click, then saw it glide open. Without stopping to think, he flicked the two switches inside.

"*Phoenix*: go faster than the speed of light!" he ordered.

The *Phoenix* paused, as if considering his

request. Then the ship's voice said, "Engaging superluminal drive . . . three . . . two . . . one . . ."

The vessel shuddered like a collapsing star. Then it leaped into the vortex at such phenomenal speed that everything blurred. When the whirling current took hold of the *Phoenix,* an earsplitting explosion crashed all around them.

CRACK-KADABOOM!

The spaceship spun and jolted and convulsed. Diesel and Selene covered their eyes. Peri held on to his armrest in a death grip, barely able to breathe.

Then everything went black.

chaos of white-hot light that rattled the entire ship.

KA-BLAM!

The colossal blast flung the *Phoenix* away from the vortex. It tumbled and whipped through space like dust in a solar wind— sideways, upside down, back to front. Thankfully, the bridge's UpRighter mechanism kept it steady, no matter what. But Peri still had to turn his back to the monitors to avoid getting dizzy. He and Selene worked frantically to get the ship under control.

Together they managed to bring the *Phoenix* safely to rest.

"Phew!" Selene said. Peri wiped his brow and smiled.

Diesel lounged against the gunnery station. "We've saved our galaxy," he boasted. "With the vortex gone, no more Xion ships can ambush the Milky Way."

Chapter 6

It was the most complete darkness Peri had ever experienced. He couldn't see the slightest gleam in the viewing panel, or the tiniest pinprick of light anywhere.

There was nothing at all.

He was thrown forward onto his astro harness, then back into his seat, left and right, up and down. A hard object he couldn't see grazed his cheek. Even as he was being flung around, he caught sight of a faint glow ahead. Seconds later, he could make things out in the dimness. A loose wrench whirled through the air toward him, only just missing his forehead.

The *Phoenix* shot out the other side of the vortex and spun around one more time to face its churning mouth. Then the vessel came to a halt. The lights blinked on, and the air pressure inside the bridge stabilized.

After a dazed pause, they all cheered. Selene punched the air: "We made it!"

"That . . . was . . . close . . ." Peri panted with relief.

Diesel patted himself all over. "Yep, I'm alive . . ." Then he grinned and shouted even louder, "*Ŏ'jhic!*"

Selene glanced around for the wrench that had fallen from her tool belt. Suddenly she grabbed Peri's arm. Peri winced in pain. He'd almost forgotten the gash the Xion alien had made with its pincher. Selene's other hand was pointing straight at the vortex. It had stopped rotating and now hung in space, a heaving, pitch-black mass. As they stared, it started to spin in the other direction, gathering speed with unbelievable force.

"NO!" Selene cried. "We're too close, we'll be sucked back in!"

Peri's hands were straining toward the control panel. "We'll just go superluminal again."

"We can't," Selene said, checking the energy gauge. "Superluminal drains the ship's energy and we can't use it again until we've had time to recharge."

The *Phoenix* shuddered under the force of the mighty vortex. They stood openmouthed and watched the vortex swirling ever faster until it seemed to reach top speed. Then it exploded into a

"I guess," Peri said. Then a thought struck him like a laser beam: they might *never* know if the Milky Way was safe. Yes, they'd destroyed the Xions' attack route, but the vortex was also their only way back home.

He sighed. They'd better face facts: this spaceship was going to be their home for some time.

Maybe forever.

Selene looked glum too. She was studying the navigation system. It showed no flight paths, no coordinates, no speed calculations . . . nothing.

"How can that be?" he asked her.

Selene shrugged. "We're in a new galaxy on the other side of the vortex. Maybe even another universe, for all we know. Wherever we are, we're in a place that hasn't yet been mapped by Earth's galactic cartographers."

Panic vibrated through Peri. He and his crew literally had no idea where they were—and neither did anybody else.

"We're cosmically lost," he groaned.

He stared hopelessly at the boundless view on the monitors. They were in a planetary system all right, but it looked totally unfamiliar. For a start, several suns were blazing in the far distance. The huge planets he could see all seemed to be in pairs, and had no moons. And there were bright nebula clouds everywhere.

"Hey!" Selene said. "What's *that*?"

A small purple orb had ejected from the hull of the *Phoenix*. It was whizzing around the constellations like a crazy robotic spaceball.

"No way!" Peri shouted excitedly. "It's the Quikmap 7000! I heard my parents talk about it once, but I didn't think they'd built the prototype yet. That little thing can chart a galaxy faster than a lightning strike."

Diesel craned his neck for a better view. They followed the orb's path on the viewing panel, which zoomed in with its millionfold magnifying lens.

Peri continued, "See, Quikmap 7000 takes thousands of infrared images that feed into the ship's navigation system. We'll have a map of our new terrain in under a minute!"

"Yeah," Diesel said, trying to sound bored. "I've known about the Quikmap all my life . . ."

Peri rolled his eyes, squared his shoulders, and said, "Listen, Your Highness: we've got to work together if we're going to survive out here. We need to get organized." He ticked off a list on his fingers: "How

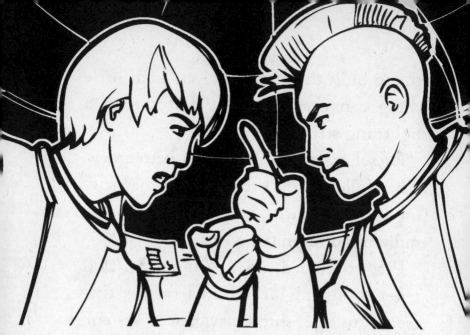

much food and water do we have onboard?
How about fuel? How long—"

"Wait a minute!" Diesel interrupted, his
band of hair bristling. "Who died and
made *you* captain? I mean, this ship just isn't
big enough for all three of us. I should
eject the pair of you into space."

"Actually," Selene replied, "it's big enough
for all of us *and* a few thousand friends." She
leaned over and studied the control panel.

"I only know a fraction of the expansion packs. But *this*"—she tapped a button—"and *this*"—she flipped a switch—"and *this*"—she clapped her hands with a flourish—"should do for now."

Peri and Diesel watched in awe as the *Phoenix* transformed itself. The egg-shaped pod expanded, growing a bunch of hallways and compartments. In every direction new portals led to unexplored areas. It was like watching a spaceship being born. Everything gleamed in the rays of the galaxy's many suns.

"That's amazing!" Peri exclaimed. "What's *in* those extensions?"

"I'll find out!" Diesel said eagerly. "I'll report back when . . . when I feel like it." He sauntered off, then called over his shoulder, "I mean, *if* I feel like it . . ."

Peri and Selene shared a look. Being lost

in space with this big-headed bozo was *not* going to be fun.

"I'll head to Engineering to assess the damage," Selene said as she pulled on her ultraviolet goggles. "I'll see if I can get superluminal working again."

"Engineering? How do you even know where that is?" Peri wondered.

"This is the *Phoenix*. If I think Engineering is down here"—she pointed at the portal farthest from Peri—"that's exactly where it will be." The portal opened with a hiss. Selene smiled. "Get it?"

Peri nodded. The ship was *designed* to help out its crew. It could sense what they needed. "Awesome!" he exclaimed.

He watched Selene leave, then turned to the Quikmap 7000 and set their course for the nearest uninhabited planet. Until they figured things out, being safe from enemy attack was their first priority. And his current plan was to hide.

He collapsed into his captain's chair. Now that he had a quiet moment, he realized his arm was throbbing. It still hurt where the alien's claw had slashed it. He took off his torn space jacket. His shirt

sleeve was stiff with dried blood, but he tugged apart the rip as best he could and looked in. It was pretty gruesome. His skin had peeled away from the bright red gash, showing the flesh and veins beneath.

But there was something else in there too. Something that pulsed with a faint blue light.

He looked closer. Wires? Tiny computer chips? His arm looked more like the inner workings of a computer than the inside of a human.

Now his own body felt alien.

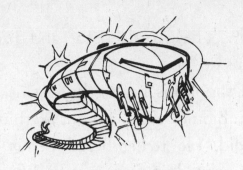

Chapter 7

Peri was totally confused. His mind raced at superluminal speed. How could he have wires in him if he was human?

Or *was* he? Could he be bionic without knowing it? Was he actually a robot programmed to behave like an Earth boy?

No. No, that can't be right, he thought, as he checked himself all over for signs—rivets, switches, any metal—that he might not have noticed before. He found nothing.

He could feel his heart pounding in his chest. "I can't be bionic!" he whispered fiercely. "I have to sleep, eat, and drink like humans do."

Peri shook his head—he just *couldn't* be bionic. Bionic beings did not *feel* things like Peri did. He remembered being happy, scared, excited, and angry in his life—man-made robots did not have emotions.

"Plus, I'm bleeding," he reassured himself. "Robots don't bleed. So I can't be *all* bionic."

There was no time to figure out anything else because, when he looked up, he saw his mom and dad. He rubbed his tired eyes. *I must be dreaming*, he thought. *Or maybe traveling through the vortex knocked us all unconscious? Maybe I'm not—*

He looked closer at his parents, smiling and nodding. They were wearing their lab coats and standing in front of a wall covered with space-o-metric diagrams. He recognized that wall and all the equipment

scattered around them. They were in their astro-lab, which, for reasons of intergalactic security, hovered in an unknown location over the Atlantic Ocean.

Peri was looking at a detailed hologram.

His mother spoke first. "Peri, if you're receiving this message, something has gone terribly wrong."

A lump caught in Peri's throat. This was a prerecorded message, and it wasn't very recent either. His father didn't have his beard, and his mother still had long hair. They were a lot younger.

Now his father was talking. He looked serious. "Son, you're the only one who can handle this mission."

"Me?" Peri said aloud. He'd only had twelve days of cadet training!

His father went on, "You see, your mother and I desperately wanted to give you the chance to escape if there was a Universal War. So we modified you." He smiled affectionately. "You're part bionic and part human. You can connect with this great ship on a human and robotic level. Your full name is Experiment, but everyone's always called you Peri for short." He gazed at Peri. "Now that you are onboard the *Phoenix*, the bionic part of you has been engaged. Son, you are *vital* to the running of the *Phoenix*. In fact, it can't function without you."

Peri felt as if the whole cosmos had been turned upside down. Then, slowly, everything started to make a kind of sense. "So *that's* why I understand how the controls work," he said.

Well, it certainly explained a lot. But it also raised about a million more questions.

He was not going to get answers, though—his parents were already giving their final recorded words of advice: "Trust your judgment," encouraged his mother. "Use all your skills," urged his father.

Then, together, they said: "We hope to see you again someday." His mother's voice trembled with emotion.

The image dissolved. Peri's parents were gone.

He was overwhelmed. He needed more answers.

Peri slipped his coverall back on. The sleeve had already mended itself, and the tear was completely gone. "I don't want the others to see my wires," he said to himself. "Nobody can know about this till I've had a chance to—"

Blip! Blip! Something was coming into focus on the viewing panel. His jaw dropped.

"Oh, no!" Peri searched frantically for the intercom button, found it, and pressed it. "Selene! Get back here!"

Tsack! Selene materialized right next to his chair. Peri jumped so high it was like he'd lost gravity.

"Don't *do* that!" he cried out in surprise. Then he looked at her in admiration. "Did you just *beam* yourself here? How?"

Selene didn't reply. She just stared at the monitor, her face turning paler and paler . . .

Without a word, she grabbed the control panel from Peri. Her fingers were a blur of speed over the keys. Then she said in a rush, "I've got to shrink the ship to a more maneuverable size, or we'll be in big trouble!"

Peri's first thought was, *But Diesel's off somewhere* . . . Before he could open his mouth, the expansion packs soundlessly retracted. Diesel tumbled back onto the bridge. He bounced to his feet, and the portal disappeared behind him.

"What the *ar'ba'h* is going on?!" he huffed. "What are you *Oorts* up to now?"

He got no reply. Selene zoomed in on the viewing panel, and all three of them gawked.

The scene was like something from the academy's 3-D battle simulations, but a zillion times more frightening. Two awesome alien warships faced off against each other. One of the vessels was snaking back and forth across the floodlit sky like an immense viper. Its reinforced hull had hundreds of

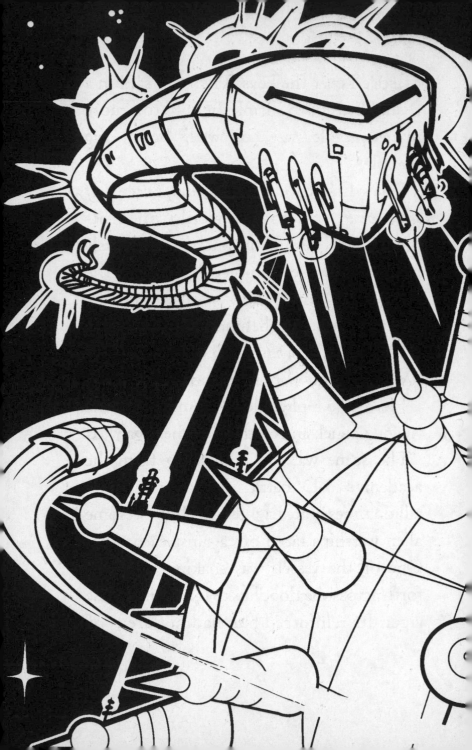

pulsing segments, each one loaded with deadly currents that rippled into the atmosphere. Even at this distance they made the *Phoenix*'s radioactivity gauge screech. The other warship was a metal orb with spikes and eyeballs and DeathRays. Peri had seen too many of these today . . .

"Xions *again!*" Diesel spat out. "Don't these guys ever stop?"

The Xions unleashed a firestorm of DeathRays at the viper ship, which hissed back jets of crimson current. The galaxy was ablaze with blinding white flashes and scorching red blasts. Steel tentacles whipped out of the Xion vessel. The viper ship writhed back, then zapped them. Chunks of tentacle whizzed past the *Phoenix*.

Peri realized their ship was completely open to attack.

"Selene!" he shouted. "Switch on the cloaking device!"

She shook her head. "It's out of order. We've got to think of something else . . ."

Peri was baffled. "Well, then let's super-luminal ourselves out of here!"

Again, she shook her head. "That's what I discovered in Engineering. The vortex damaged our ship. I don't know how badly yet, but those functions aren't working."

"So we're a sitting target?" Diesel yelled. "I thought you were supposed to be a crack mechanic!"

All of a sudden the viper ship twisted around to face the *Phoenix*. Every one of the Xion ship's eyeballs swiveled toward them as well.

Then, as Peri, Selene, and Diesel watched, both warships readied and aimed their weapons . . . right at *them*.

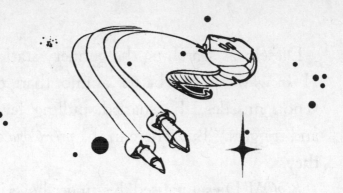

Chapter 8

The hull of the viper ship was pulsing with deadly currents. The hatches of the Xion warcraft gaped open, each one revealing a loaded DeathRay pulverizer.

The *Phoenix* was about to be wiped out.

Everyone sprang into action. Peri grabbed the control panel and twisted an expansion knob. "Selene!" he said urgently. "Get back to Engineering! You've got to give us more speed somehow, or make us invisible!" The girl saluted and sprinted toward the corridor that was just appearing.

Diesel was searching the gunnery station. "I *know* we've got better ammo than the xenon missiles," he snarled, pulling levers and triggers. "But where in the *prrrip'chiq* are they?"

BOOM! Diesel paused, his finger hovering over the last button. The Xion ship was firing at them. *BOOM!* Peri stood still, his eyes warily scanning the monitors. He couldn't see the enemies' rockets. An eerie silence fell, like the calm before a meteor storm.

As if in a daze, Peri threw a switch to activate the SeeAll. Instantly, the viewing panel blacked out everything—planets, stars, spaceships—except the two enemy stealth charges. Both were hurtling on a direct course for the *Phoenix*. They were invisible to the naked eye.

"Gotcha, you Xion sneaks!" Peri cried.

He seized the Nav-wheel, and in one swift

movement steered the spaceship out of their line of fire. The stealth charges raced past into the darkness.

Boom! Boom! Boom! Immediately, dozens of new stealth charges appeared on the SeeAll, alongside tons of DeathRay lasers.

Peri flexed his fingers. This was going to be like bumper-car pods, but even messier . . .

"All engines firing, Captain!" Selene called up on the intercom. "We've got more speed, but no superluminal yet."

Peri couldn't reply. He was counting down to his next countermaneuver, "Three . . . two . . ."

His hand froze. What looked like a massive wave was sweeping over the map on the SeeAll. The stealth charges detonated midflight. The DeathRay lasers splintered into harmless sparks.

Peri's mouth fell open. "But . . . ," he stammered.

Diesel snickered. "I found the sonic boom and sent our Xion friends a whopping wave of noise!" he said. He patted a large zip-dial that had sprung up from his console. He was still guffawing when he stuck his fingers in his ears. Peri looked at him, puzzled.

"What are you doing that for?" he asked.

Diesel shrugged. "No reason," he replied. Seconds later, a head-splitting roar washed over them, practically lifting Peri out of his seat. It was so loud it was like being inside a supercharged turbo engine. He gawked at Diesel. He could see the half-Martian laughing and laughing until blue tears ran down his cheeks. Diesel mouthed, "Feedback!"

But Peri couldn't hear a thing.

All at once the *Phoenix* began pitching and rocking as a new round of Xion lasers smacked into its defense shield. Direct hits! Peri could see from the control panel that the shield's protective power was dropping to dangerous levels. The bridge lights flashed red. Peri guessed an alarm was going off too. Diesel's smirk was gone. While the sonic boom reloaded, the gunner fought back with xenon missiles.

"If the viper ship attacks us now, we're history!" Peri said loudly. He was still deaf, and his head felt fuzzy. "We've got to let them know we're on their side against those Xion bullies."

Peri felt a rush of air as Selene materialized next to him. Then he saw her shout, "Heat-seeking rocket!" and she shoved him out of the way.

Peri watched as Selene deactivated the SeeAll and spun thermo-dials to rapidly cool the *Phoenix*. On the monitors he could see that the rocket had been launched from the viper ship.

Peri groaned. "They're the enemies of our enemies. That should make them our friends! I mean, we've been trying to *help* them . . ."

The *Phoenix* bucked and swerved. Selene was accelerating hard to stay ahead of the rocket. Peri's eardrums popped and his head cleared. He had an idea.

"My turn!" he said, grabbing the controls.

Diesel was still at the gunnery station, *rat-tat-tat*-ing some weapon or other toward the rocket, without success.

Peri steeled himself and then charged the *Phoenix* right at the Xion warship. The vessel flew so effortlessly under his command that it felt like an extension of his own body. He headed into the lightning storm of pulverizer beams and stealth charges. Selene called out directions: "Go left!"

"Pull up NOW!"

"Bank right!"

With her help, Peri dodged everything the aliens threw at them. He skimmed across the spikes and whipped around the eyeballs, until he dropped the *Phoenix* like a falling star right behind the Xion warship.

The heat-seeking rocket was fooled. Instead of the *Phoenix*, it homed in on the nearest molten-red pulverizer. There was an eye-scorching flash, an immense *BANG*, and then a mass of swirling debris. The Xion warship was obliterated.

Peri punched the air. "Nice work, crew!"

The viper ship seemed to be retreating. Its crimson hull had stopped pulsing, and its thrashing tail finally lay still. Peri held his breath. Maybe everything was going to be okay.

"Are we safe now?" Selene whispered.

The measured voice of the *Phoenix* intervened. "Attention: receiving data from alien source." Bizarre symbols began to scroll down the monitors.

Peri looked at the others. "Any idea what that means?"

Selene shook her head. "Not a clue."

Diesel shrugged. "Just when I *get* a word or two," he said, "it scrambles again."

Selene pressed a few buttons to try to

decipher the alien message. Then she gulped.

"What does it say?" Peri demanded. He had a feeling it meant even more trouble.

"Uh . . ." Selene's voice was nervous. "I think it says, 'Prepare . . . Prepare—'"

A harsh yellow light engulfed them. Peri squeezed his eyes shut, but the rays pierced through his lids and made him cover his face. Then, just as quickly, the light was gone. The three of them blinked cautiously. Their eyes widened in surprise.

The *Phoenix* seemed to be in a gigantic box. Red light was radiating from the distant walls. Maybe heat too, because blue sweat was trickling down Diesel's face. Peri could feel his Expedition Wear sticking to his skin. Through the 360-monitor, he peered into the dimness, but he couldn't see any openings. All he could make out

were hundreds of crates and boxes: ammu-
nition, spare parts, and a vast glass tank
teeming with gross bugs.

They were in the cargo bay of the viper
ship!

"Uh..." Selene finished her sentence:
" 'Prepare to be beamed aboard'!"

Chapter 9

"*Ephguxoopkeegok!*"

An alien voice was broadcasting over the *Phoenix*'s intercom. Everyone jumped. It spoke in a harsh, booming language with sharp clicking sounds. The message was repeated again and again. It sounded more threatening each time.

Peri felt under his chin for the slight bulge of the SpeakEasy computer chip. All cadets, in their first week at the IF Academy, had a SpeakEasy implanted. As he tuned in the translation device, the crackling static made his skull vibrate. Then he found the right wavelength.

"Set your language controls to frequency 11.08.68," he told his crew.

Diesel followed his order. Selene pulled a battered SpeakEasy from her tool belt and tied it under her chin. Now all three of them could understand the booming alien announcement: "Exit your ship! Come out with your hands up!"

"We have no choice," Peri said flatly. "We have to surrender." He shut down the ship's accelerator modules. Then he quickly ran an air-quality test on the cargo bay.

The computer's response was surprising: "Safe for you to breathe—but quite" . . . something. Peri couldn't understand the last word.

Selene pressed a couple of buttons. Mechanical arms shot out of the walls and dressed her in Expedition Wear. Then they all marched down the corridor to meet their fate.

Diesel and Selene flanked Peri as the exit hatch appeared. The door swung open and a ramp glided down. They raised their hands.

As they stepped outside, the smell hit Peri like a punch in the nose. The hot air reeked of something terrible, like rotting food or

filthy animals—only much, much worse. Selene gagged. Peri took tiny breaths through his mouth. Diesel stuffed two wads of Eterni-chew gum up his nostrils and smirked.

As they walked slowly down the ramp, the smell became overwhelming. But when Peri finally saw the aliens, the sight took his mind off everything else. A high-ranking officer with rows of gleaming medals pinned to his uniform was waiting. He was surrounded by more than a dozen armed guards. And they were like no species Peri had ever seen before.

Their necks were twice as long as a human's, with two big lumps sticking out of their wrinkled flesh. The front of each lump was covered with a fine mesh that looked like a loudspeaker. Peri nodded to himself. *No wonder their voices boom!*

The creatures had crimson skin the same

color as their ship, with splotches of black around their eyes and ears.

The officer advanced, and the guards followed. The aliens' bodies were hard and muscular, almost human in shape. But their lower backs had hideous humps, which made them stoop as they walked. Their long powerful arms had two elbows that bent in opposite directions. Peri was pretty sure they'd be impossible to beat in cosmic combat—or arm wrestling. Even for Diesel. Besides, he and his friends were outnumbered four to one, *and* the guards carried what looked like electromagnetic zapsters. Fighting them was out of the question.

The two groups stood facing each other. The aliens had mouths but no lips or teeth. From each jaw flickered a rough-looking black tongue, which Peri somehow knew could reach really far.

"*Mza-kåk, Mza'pûu!*" Diesel mumbled so only Peri and Selene could hear. "Ugly sons of ugly mothers of ugly grand-fathers . . ." He went back another five generations. Selene snickered nervously.

Peri stammered the IF motto: "P-peace in Space." Or that's what his brain said. His SpeakEasy translated it into a harsh jumble of grunts and clicks.

"Welcome!" the officer replied in English. His tone was friendly—but either his language device needed adjusting or he always spoke as if he was barking orders. "Be at ease! We must thank you! You helped destroy our enemy!"

Peri's mouth dropped open in surprise. He immediately wished it hadn't, because it let in more foul-smelling air. A friendly greeting was the last thing he had expected from aliens as ugly as these.

"Friends!" the alien continued. "Take down your hands!"

Peri lowered his hands. He felt relieved. "The Xions are attacking our galaxy too," he explained, breathing as little as possible. "It was an ambush."

"Awful!" the general responded. "Awful! I will introduce myself!" He smacked his hands together over his head, making everyone flinch. "I salute you!" he declared. Peri thought there was a faint sneer on his face, but it was difficult to tell.

"General Rouwgim!" the alien bellowed. "From planet Meigwor! In the Ubi Galaxy! And the name of your galaxy?"

Peri blinked. "Sorry?"

"The name of your galaxy?!"

Diesel butted in. "The Milky Way, General."

"It is good!" General Rouwgim shouted.

"The Sun, the Earth, the Pluto, the Mars!"

He started to walk around the *Phoenix*. Peri followed a few steps behind. Half the guards went with them, and the rest surrounded Diesel and Selene. Peri looked back. Selene gave him a tight smile that said, *We're okay. Let's just see what happens.*

"It is good!" The alien leered. His tongue waggled in his mouth. "We Meigwors are at war with Xion! They have fuel! So much fuel! We Meigwors are running out of fuel! The Xions do not share! If we Meigwors have no fuel, we will die!"

Peri was listening and nodding. But he felt uneasy, and it wasn't just the smell. Or the fact that one of those horrible stink-bugs had scuttled out of the teeming tank and was making its way across the floor. There was something strange about the way General Rouwgim kept inspecting him and his crew and the *Phoenix*. His beady eyes, his barked commands, his armed guards . . .

Of course, it made sense for Peri and his crew to be allies with the Meigwors. But even though he couldn't put his finger on it, he knew something wasn't right.

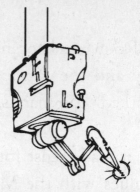

Chapter 10

Without warning, General Rouwgim's black tongue lashed out like a whip. Before Peri could react, it shot back into the alien's mouth. The stinkbug was stuck to it, struggling with all its many legs.

"Excuse me!" the general gurgled. "I have a sweet tooth!"

And he swallowed the bug whole.

Peri cringed in horror. General Rouwgim was circling the *Phoenix* as if nothing had happened. Peri could see the bug thrashing wildly as it made its way down the alien's throat. By the time they'd returned to Diesel and Selene, Peri had got ahold of himself.

"You are awfully young," Rouwgim hollered, "to be pilots of own ship!"

"Actually," Diesel said in his gruffest voice, "we're a pretty experienced crew."

Peri was confused. What was Diesel talking about? The gunner gave him a sly look. Then Peri got it: they must not look weak in front of the Meigwors.

"You see, General," Peri bluffed, "we're older than we look. People in our galaxy are quite small."

"But we're tough!" Diesel added, flexing his muscles. "I blew up a Xion warship while we were being sucked into a vortex. And *then* we wiped out the vortex just by flying through it."

"It is good!" Rouwgim roared and

clapped. "And your ship! It is magnificent! But was it damaged in your battles?"

Peri hesitated. Was it safe to let the general know the truth? Then he realized that they weren't going anywhere without the Meigwors' help. "Yes," he admitted. "The accelerators and the cloaking device are broken."

Rouwgim's eyes shone. He looked at them sharply. "We Meigwors battle the Xions for years!" he yelled. "We Meigwors could use a crack team like you!"

"Thank you, General," Peri said politely. "But we really have to get home. We've got to crush the Xions in the Milky Way."

Rouwgim ignored him. "But Xion has captured our Meigwor prince!" he shouted. "We help you mend damaged ship! We help you return to the Milky Way! But first you help *us* find our Meigwor prince and bring him home!"

Peri turned to the others. Selene frowned and whispered, "I think it's our only option. And who knows, it might be good training before we go back home . . ."

Diesel muttered, "Just remember what General Pegg said about keeping me safe . . ."

Peri studied the floor. It was a tough decision. General Pegg *had* ordered him to get Diesel to safety. But accepting Rouwgim's offer was the only way of getting the ship repaired. He looked up and said calmly, "It's a deal, General." When they shook hands, Peri felt as if his fingers were being crushed in a vice.

"I dispatch my best ship fixers!" Rouwgim barked.

"Excellent." Peri rubbed his flattened hand. "Our engineer will supervise."

Selene marched over to the *Phoenix*. A fully equipped test-and-repair station descended

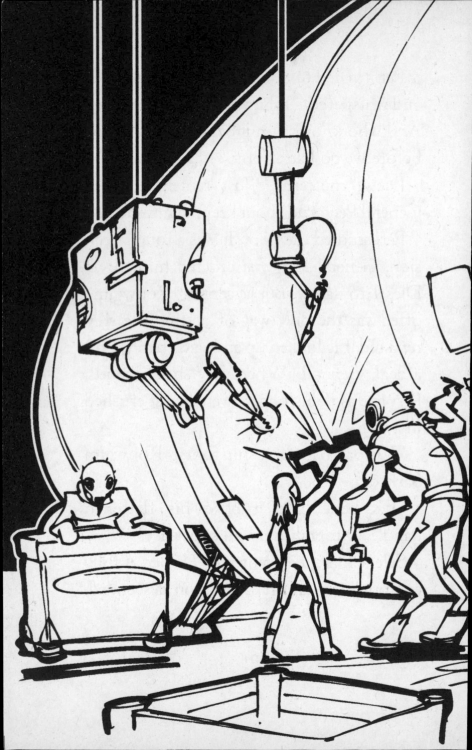

from its hull. Bright 3-D images of the engine networks sprang up. The Meigwor mechanics wheeled up a crate of spare parts and tools, and set about their work under Selene's strict instructions.

"Your ship be ready in the morning!" Rouwgim promised. "Now we celebrate victory."

"We're very grateful." Peri had prepared his next speech. "But I'm sure you only have war rations onboard," he said smoothly. "We won't take advantage of your hospitality by eating your food. We'll eat and sleep on the *Phoenix.*"

The alien looked relieved. "You are real warrior! You consider your allies!"

Peri stifled a grin. Now Rouwgim could satisfy his sweet tooth all he wanted. *And we won't have to eat stinkbugs!*

The general and his troops moved off to

their command station. Selene gave some more orders to the mechanics, then rejoined Peri and Diesel. Together they climbed back into the *Phoenix*.

Peri suddenly felt more tired and hungry than he'd ever felt in his life. Thankfully, a chill-storage unit had appeared on the ship's bridge. It was stuffed with bottles of Saturn Soda, astro-meals, and spacebars in all flavors: Mars, Saturn, Neptune, Jupiter . . .

Once Peri and Selene had finished eating, they watched Diesel wash down his ninth spacebar with his eleventh soda. His band of hair slowly drifted from side to side, showing he was full and content.

"Those mechanics are good," Selene said. "They'll fix the *Phoenix*." Then she made a face. "But I think Rouwgim is planning something."

"Definitely," Peri agreed. "But what?" He was trying to piece it all together: *Xion . . . Meigwor . . . kidnapped prince . . . war for fuel . . . what kind of fuel?* But his worn-out brain was as slow as the jumbo jet he'd once seen in a history book.

Diesel burped loudly. "I say we just take the *Phoenix* and run."

"You mean," Selene asked after a pause, "we only *pretend* to help rescue this prince?"

Diesel sniggered. "Yep, we go superluminal, and leave them gazing at our vapor trail!"

Peri shifted uneasily. "But they're repairing our ship for us."

Diesel snorted. "*Af-kyot!* C'mon! We'll still be fighting the Xions, just in our galaxy, not in theirs."

"He's right," Selene said firmly. "The Meigwors give me the creeps. The sooner we get out of here, the better."

Peri stood up and rubbed his eyes. Saving the Milky Way was obviously more important than intergalactic manners. "Okay, it's agreed," he said. "We escape at the first opportunity."

When the crew turned around, they saw that three floating sleep bays had materialized. Peri clambered into his bunk and heard the others do the same. He felt the covers pull themselves over him and tuck him in. Diesel began snoring before the lights had even dimmed.

Early the next morning, Peri and his crew bolted down a breakfast of spacecakes and hot Comet Koko. Then Selene slipped on her tool belt. Diesel shoved some Eterni-chew gum in his mouth. Peri straightened his spacesuit.

"Everyone ready?" he asked. When they

gave him the thumbs-up, he took a deep breath and led them down the ramp. General Rouwgim and his guards were already waiting for them.

The general briefed Peri about their mission: free the Meigwor prince from his Xion prison and bring him home. "Simple!" he barked. Peri nodded. Although he felt bad about accepting the Meigwors' help and then running off, deep down he knew it was the right decision.

Now he just wanted to get going.

"You have good luck!" Rouwgim commanded, as they stood together outside the *Phoenix*. "And one thing more! A new crew member for your mission!"

A burly alien stepped forward. His massive chest was crisscrossed with ammo belts. Around his waist was a snakeskin belt loaded with weapons and gadgets, some of which Peri had never seen before. Hanging next to a set of zirconium grenades were two studded tubes that glowed deathly crimson, and a vial of smoky liquid.

"Uh . . . that won't be necessary," Peri said hastily. "I already have an engineer and a gunner. That's all I need."

"Otto goes with you!" the general bellowed. This time, there was no doubt he was giving a direct order. "Otto help you

to fight! And Selene," he added slyly, "help you to come back! Because she stays here with us until you return!"

Peri stepped in front of Selene. "No way!" he said defiantly. But instantly two guards shoved their zapsters in his face and pulled Selene away. Diesel crouched in the cosmic-combat attack position. He was ready to launch himself at the general.

"Diesel, stop!" Selene shouted. "Don't make it worse!" Diesel growled but stood at case. Rouwgim smirked, though he looked a little shaken.

"General, give me your word that you won't harm her!" Peri demanded.

"Get us our prince," Rouwgim replied, "and no one gets hurt!"

Peri turned to Selene. "I promise we'll get the prince as soon as we can and come back for you."

Diesel grunted his agreement. "See you around," he said.

Selene shook off the guards' hands and stood up straight. She looked determined. "If you ever find yourself staring death in the face," she said quickly, "press the blue helix on the control panel."

The door of the *Phoenix* swung open. Peri waved good-bye to Selene. Diesel nodded at her. Then the two boys walked up the ramp. Otto lumbered after them.

As soon as they were on the bridge, the alien squeezed his massive body into the captain's chair and then stretched out his double-jointed arm to the control panel.

Peri was taken aback. Who did this giant dumboid think he was? He snapped his fingers, and the panel glided over to him.

"Out!" Diesel growled at Otto. "You're not the captain!" He jerked his thumb toward Selene's chair. The alien spewed out some grunts and clicks, but he moved over anyway.

Peri settled himself in the captain's chair. Then he focused his eyes on the viewing panel, gripped the Nav-wheel, and activated the launch sequence. With a perfect maneuver, he directed the vessel out of the viper ship's cargo bay and up into the unknown.

As the *Phoenix* shot into space, Peri vowed to himself: *I'll get us all back home . . . somehow . . . someday . . .*

How will Peri and Diesel
rescue Prince Onix ?

And can they trust the Meigwors?

Find out in

Read on for a sneak peek . . .

The vessel ahead of them entered the space-highway ramp, and the *Phoenix* glided to a stop behind a barricade of pulsing red light. An announcement from the toll taker interrupted him: "Prepare to be inspected. Approach slowly."

The Nav-wheel was slippery with ice, but Peri guided the *Phoenix* toward the striped guard pod with expert skill.

Durrr-ing! The com-screen rose from the console and flashed into life. A Xion appeared. He wore a bright-blue uniform, braided with pink, and a scarlet cap.

"This is Toll Taker Xerallon." A beam of purple light pulsed through the bridge. "The following fines have been added to your toll: crossing the Cos-Moat without permission, not using proper drawbridge protocol, and endangering local wildlife. State your name and your reasons for visiting Xion."

Peri gulped. He could have kicked himself. He should have thought of a cover story. "I . . . I . . . ," he spluttered.

"Peace in Space, Toll Taker Xerallon," Diesel said. "We apologize for our rude behavior. We're astro-nomads. We need extra fuel as well as repairs to our Nav-system. My pilot is quite useless without a navigation computer telling him where to go. Last week, he almost flew us into a moon. We were lucky to crash into your lovely Cos-Moat."

The screen was icing up, but Peri could see the toll taker nod. "Your ship's certainly a relic from a technology-stunted solar system. I'm surprised that junk can fly."

Peri wanted to glare at the toll taker. His ship wasn't junk. His parents had helped make the *Phoenix* better than anything in the universe. But arguing would only endanger the mission, so he kept quiet.

"Yes, you're right, of course," Diesel told the guard. "It's almost embarrassing to fly—practically useless."

Peri was impressed. Diesel was cool under pressure. It must have been his upbringing as the emperor's son—he knew exactly how to deal with the toll taker.

"Access granted," said the toll taker. "Please beam over payment."

"Payment?" Peri whispered to Diesel. "What are we . . . ?"

"Certainly, officer," said Diesel, cutting Peri off. "How would you like your payment?"

"Our scanners have already picked items of value."

Peri held his breath, worried about what the Xions wanted to take. White ice crystals had formed over the screen. When he scraped them away and saw the InfoBox, he almost laughed.

> IDENTIFIED: plastic storage devices and rich organic fertilizer.

"Peri," Diesel whispered. "What's 'rich organic fertilizer'?"

"Umm . . ." Peri paused. "I think they want plastic recycling bins and the contents of our space-toilets."